TALKING IS
NOT
MY THING

ROSE ROBBINS is the author of *Me and My Sister* (Eerdmans), a companion to *Talking Is Not My Thing.* She has a master of arts in children's book illustration from the Cambridge School of Art and was a runner-up for Hachette UK's Carmelite Prize in 2017. Rose grew up with an autistic brother, an experience that informs and shapes her writing. She serves as an ambassador with Inclusive Minds, an organization that promotes quality representation in children's literature, and she has written and drawn extensively about neurodiversity issues. Rose lives in Nottingham, UK. Follow her on Instagram @roserobbinsuk and visit her website at roserobbins.co.uk.

For Rowland

ACKNOWLEDGMENTS

I owe an extraordinary debt to the people whom I have approached for guidance while writing this book: Lilo, Frances, and Carly.
In particular, I would like to thank Dr. Rebecca Butler for her continual advice and support throughout the production of this book.

— R. R.

First published in the United States in 2020
by Eerdmans Books for Young Readers,
an imprint of Wm. B. Eerdmans Publishing Co.
Grand Rapids, Michigan

www.eerdmans.com/youngreaders

First published in Great Britain in 2020
by Scallywag Press Ltd., London
Text and illustration copyright © 2020 Rose Robbins

29 28 27 26 25 24 23 22 21 20   1 2 3 4 5 6 7 8 9

Library of Congress Cataloging-in-Publication Data

Names: Robbins, Rose, author.
Title: Talking is not my thing / Rose Robbins.
Description: Grand Rapids : Eerdmans Books for Young Readers, [2020] |
    Audience: Ages 3-7. | Summary: A girl with autism who almost never
    speaks demonstrates how easily she communicates with her brother and
    grandmother through facial expressions, gestures, flashcards, and
    drawings.
Identifiers: LCCN 2020000612 | ISBN 9780802855497 (hardcover)
Subjects: CYAC: Selective mutism—Fiction. | Brothers and sisters—Fiction.
    | Autism—Fiction.
Classification: LCC PZ7.1.R583 Tal 2020 | DDC [E]—dc23
LC record available at https://lccn.loc.gov/2020000612

TALKING IS NOT MY THING

ROSE ROBBINS

EERDMANS BOOKS FOR YOUNG READERS • GRAND RAPIDS, MICHIGAN

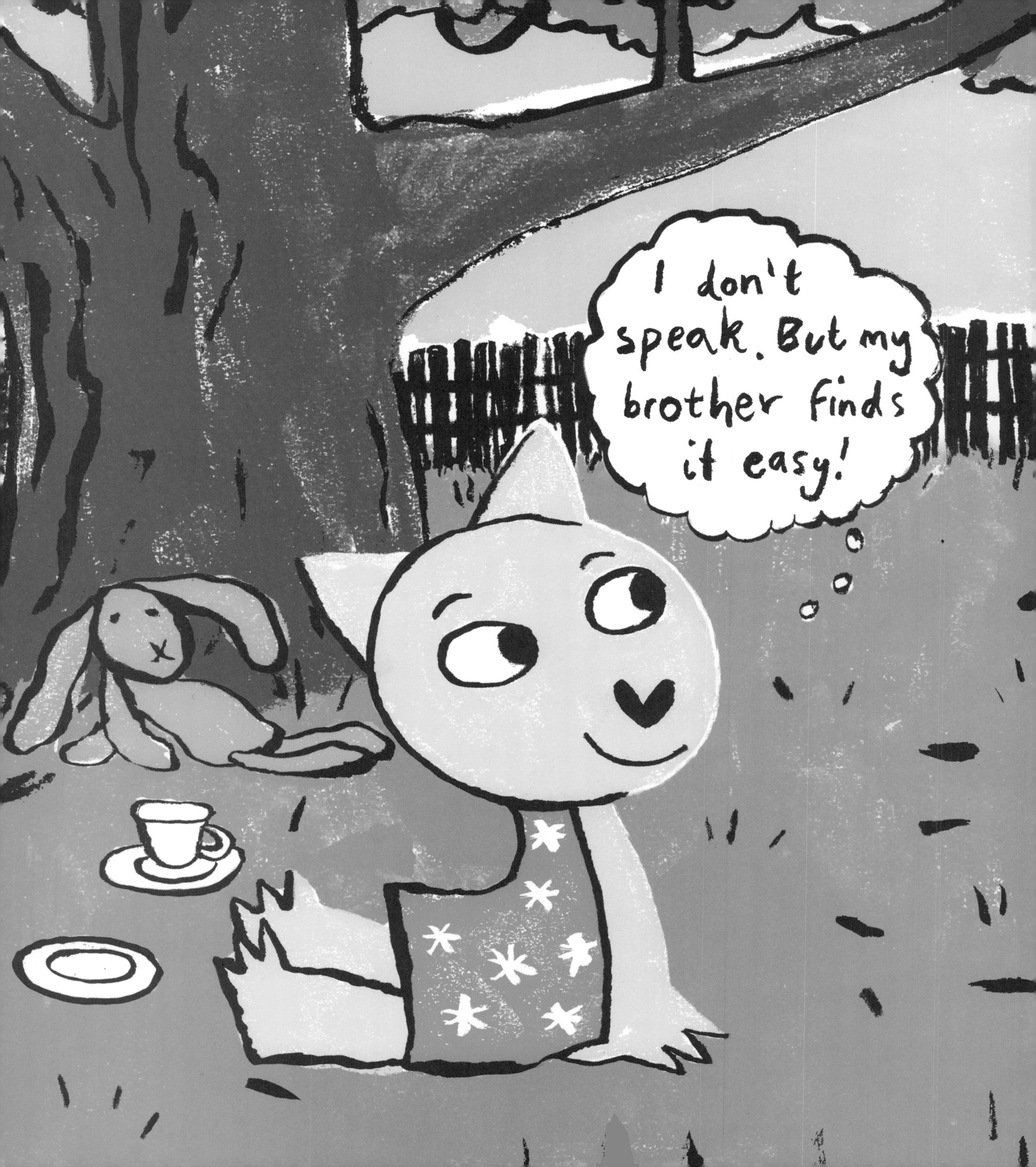
I don't speak. But my brother finds it easy!

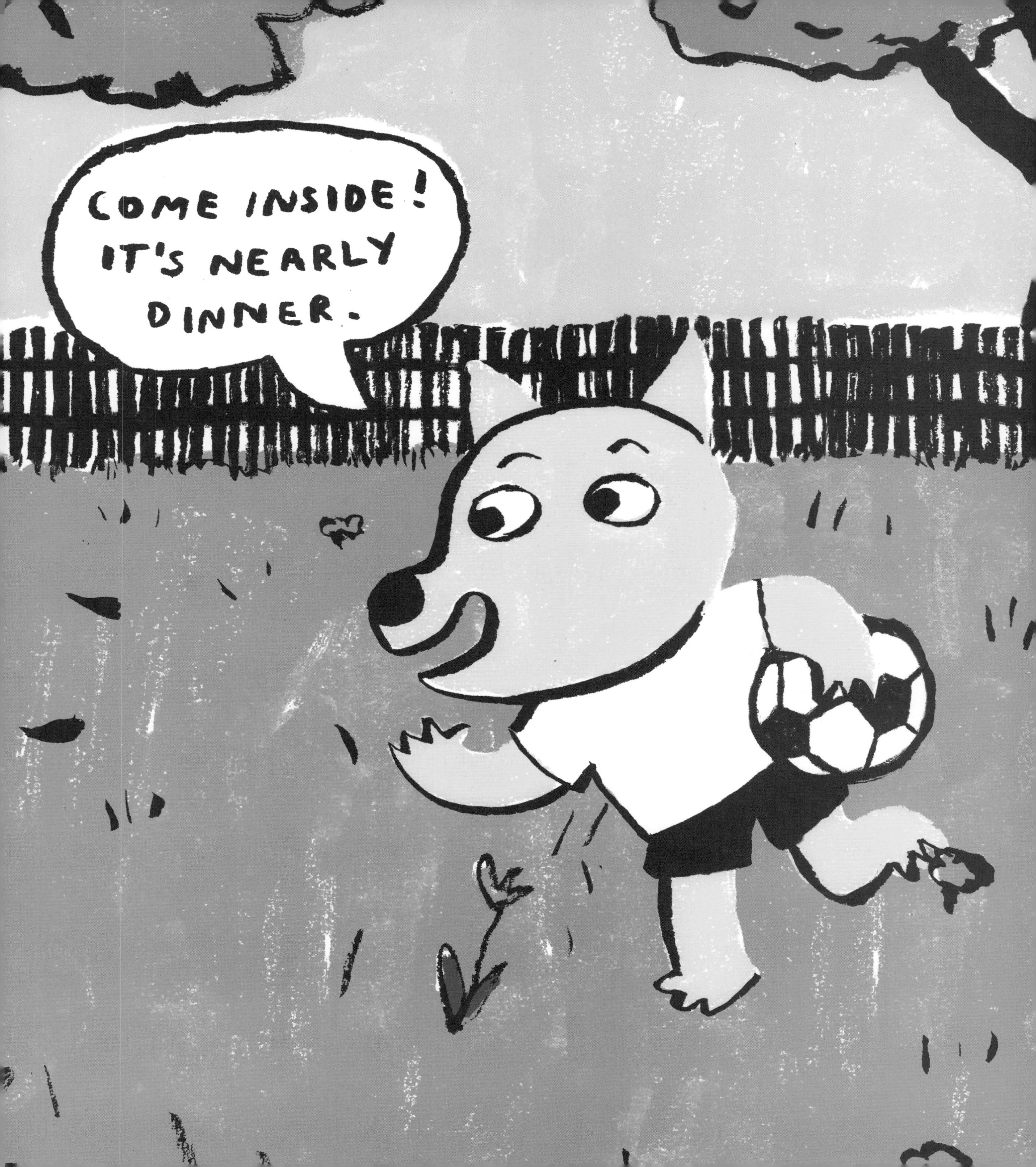
COME INSIDE! IT'S NEARLY DINNER.

But I still like to feel included.
THAT WAS YUMMY! LET'S GO AND WATCH TV WITH GRANDMA!

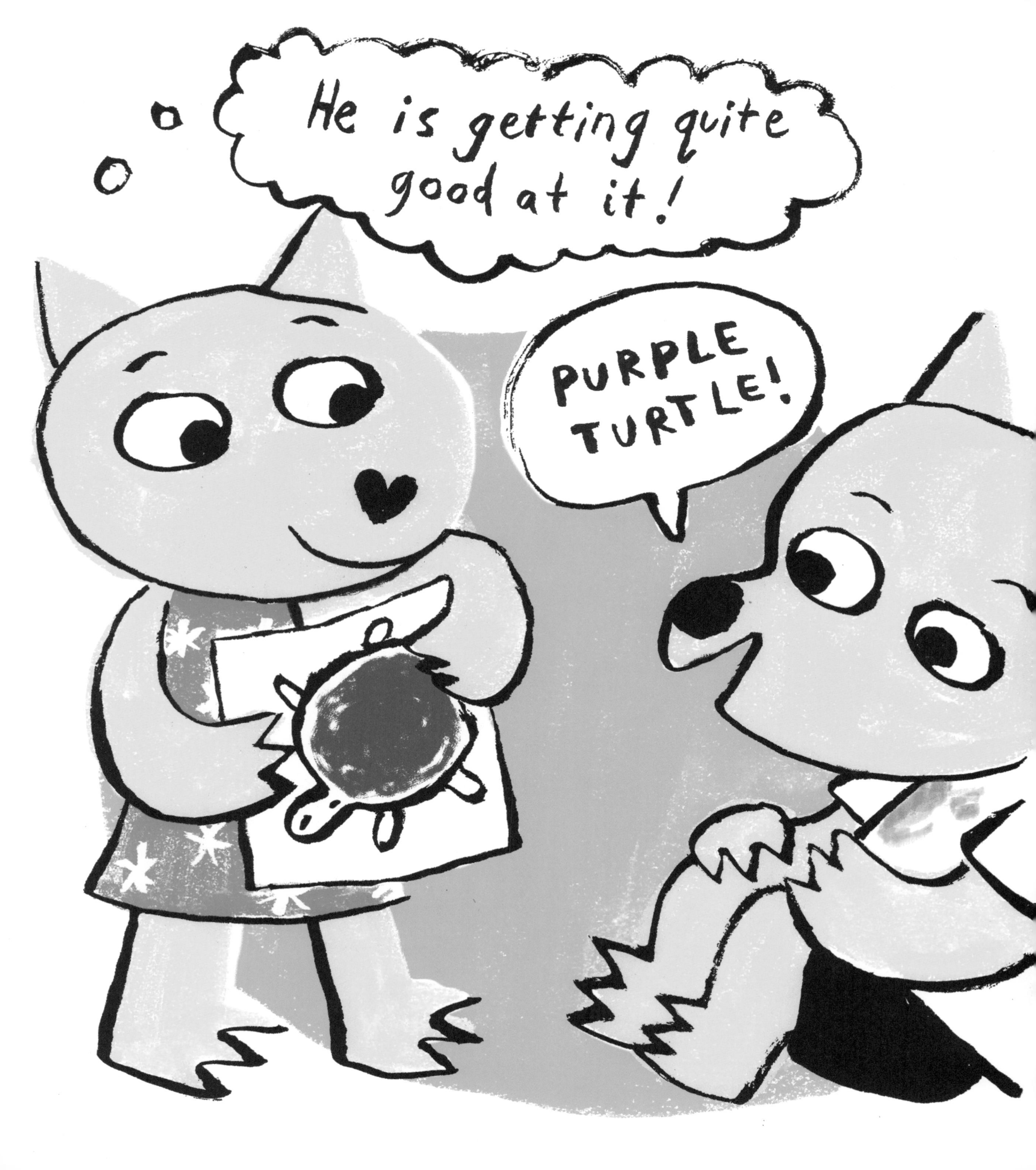
He is getting quite good at it!
PURPLE TURTLE!

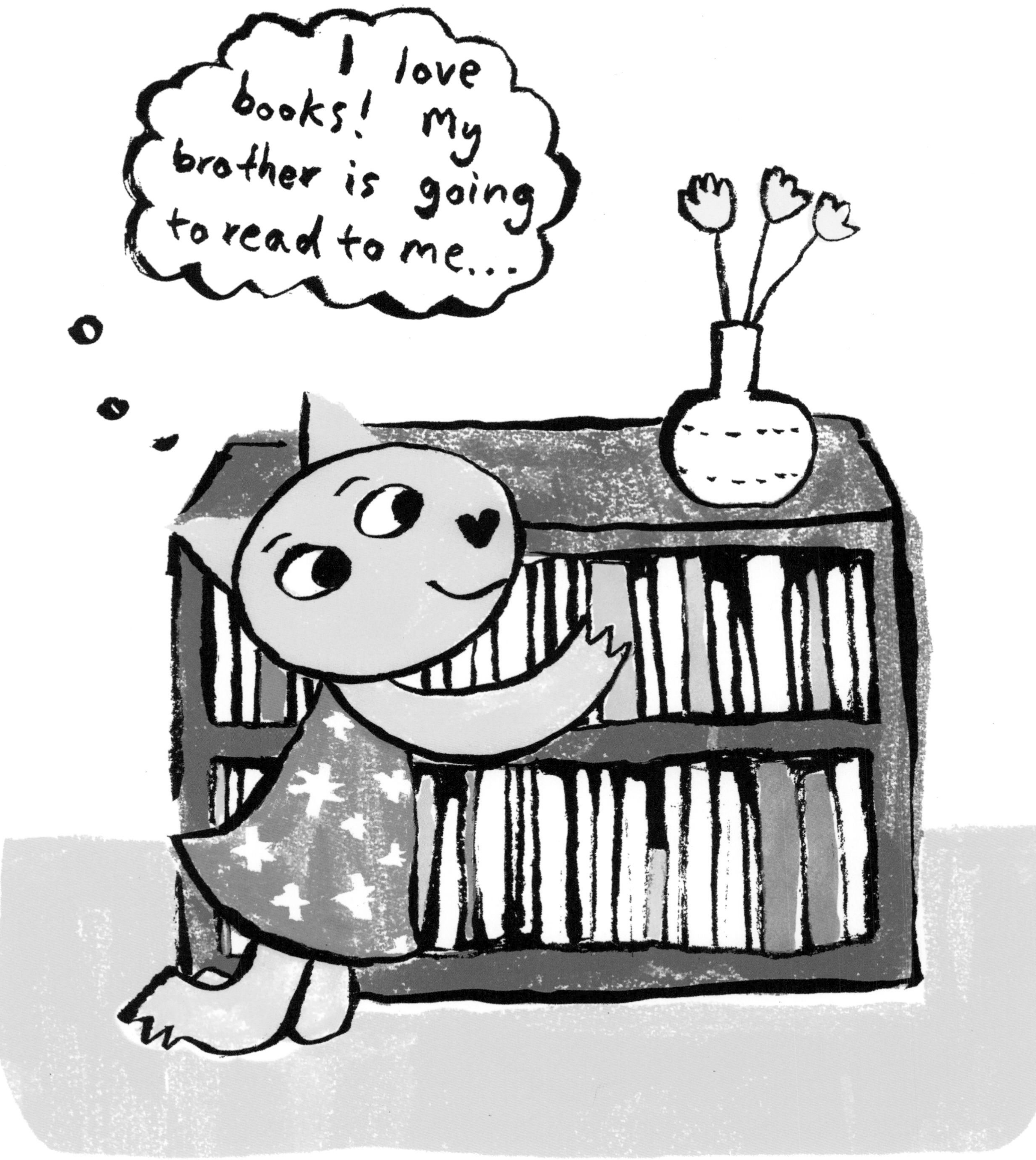
I love books! My brother is going to read to me...

BRUSH
BRUSH
BRUSH

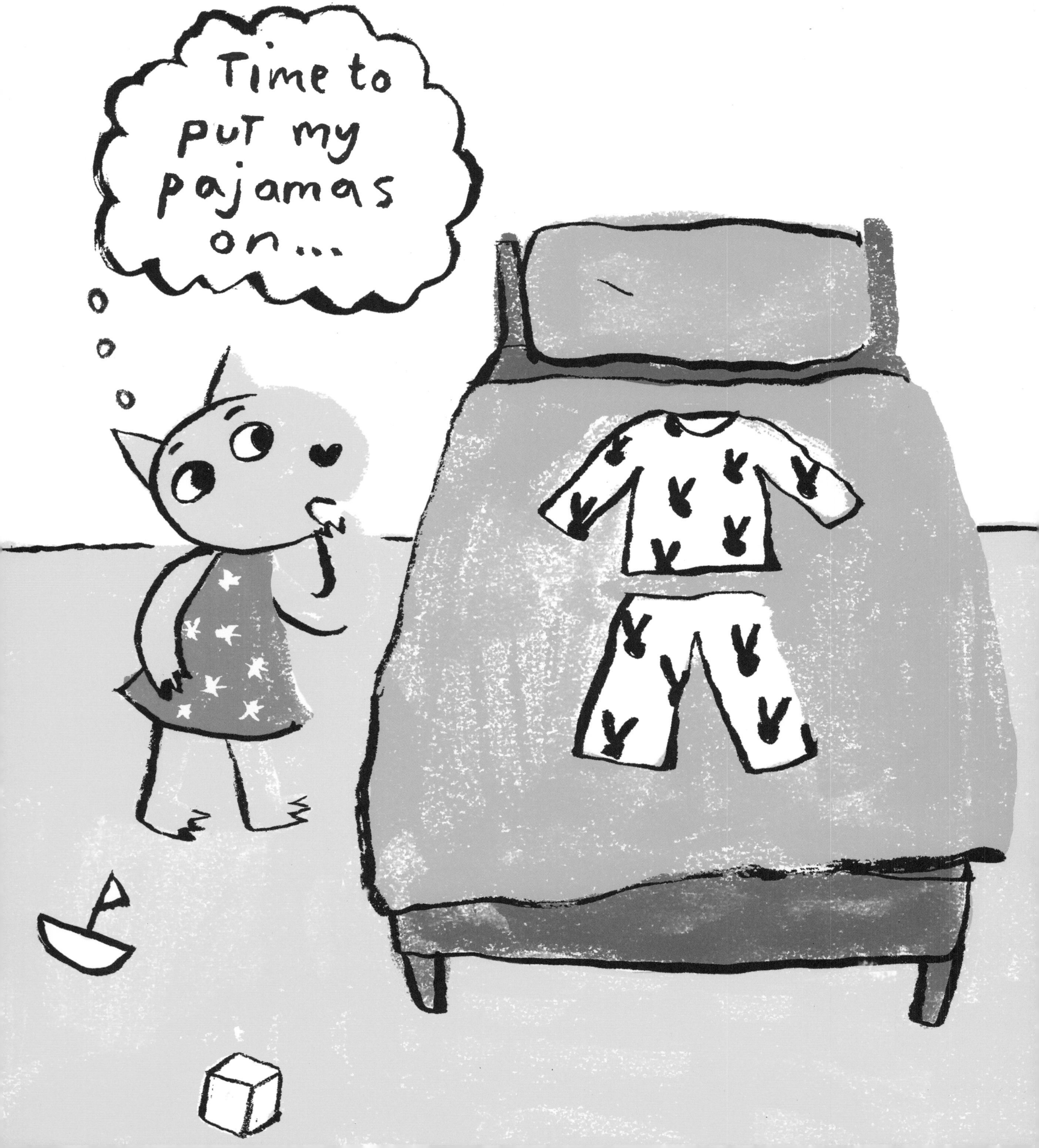
Time to put my pajamas on...

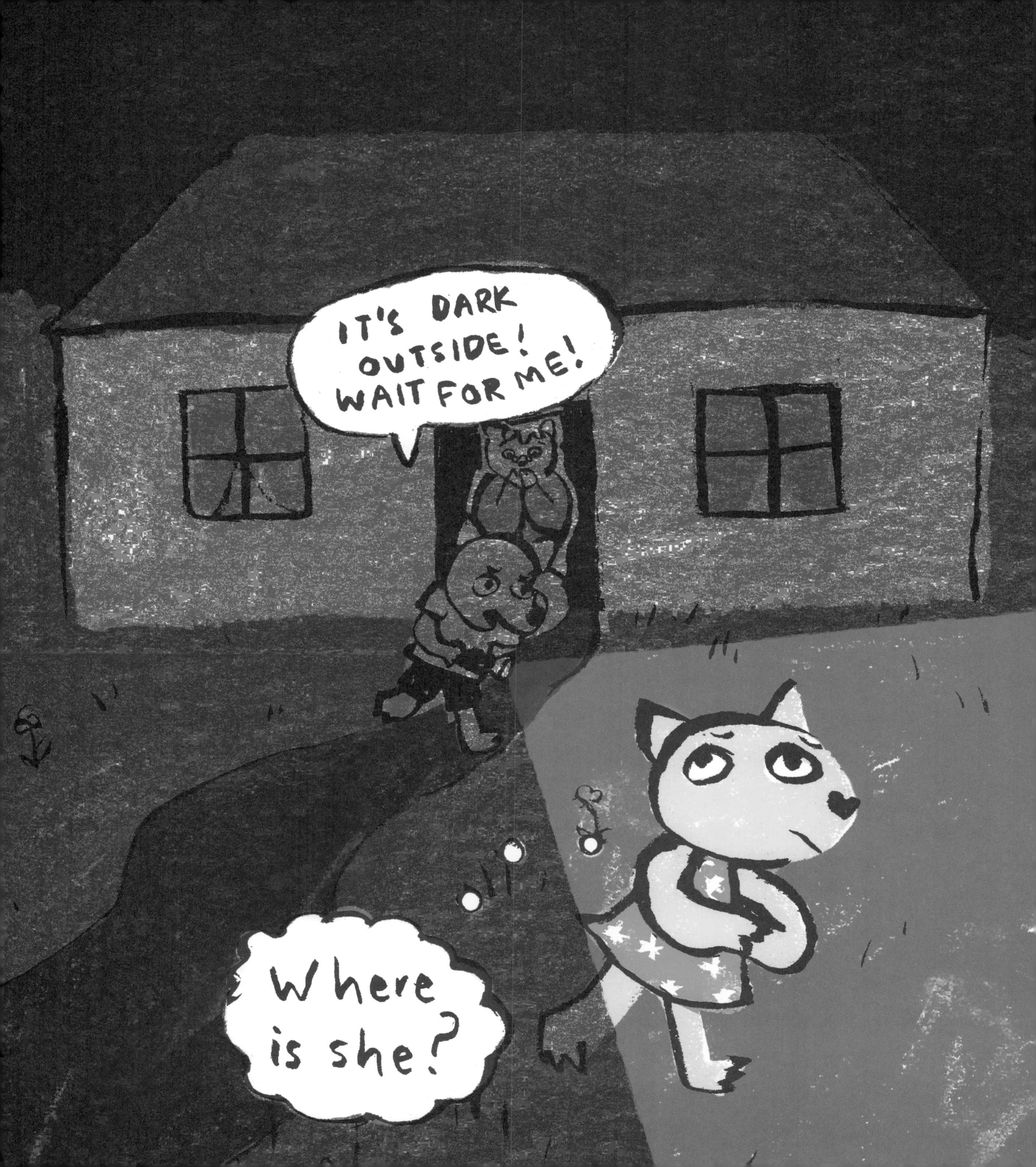
IT'S DARK OUTSIDE! WAIT FOR ME!
Where is she?

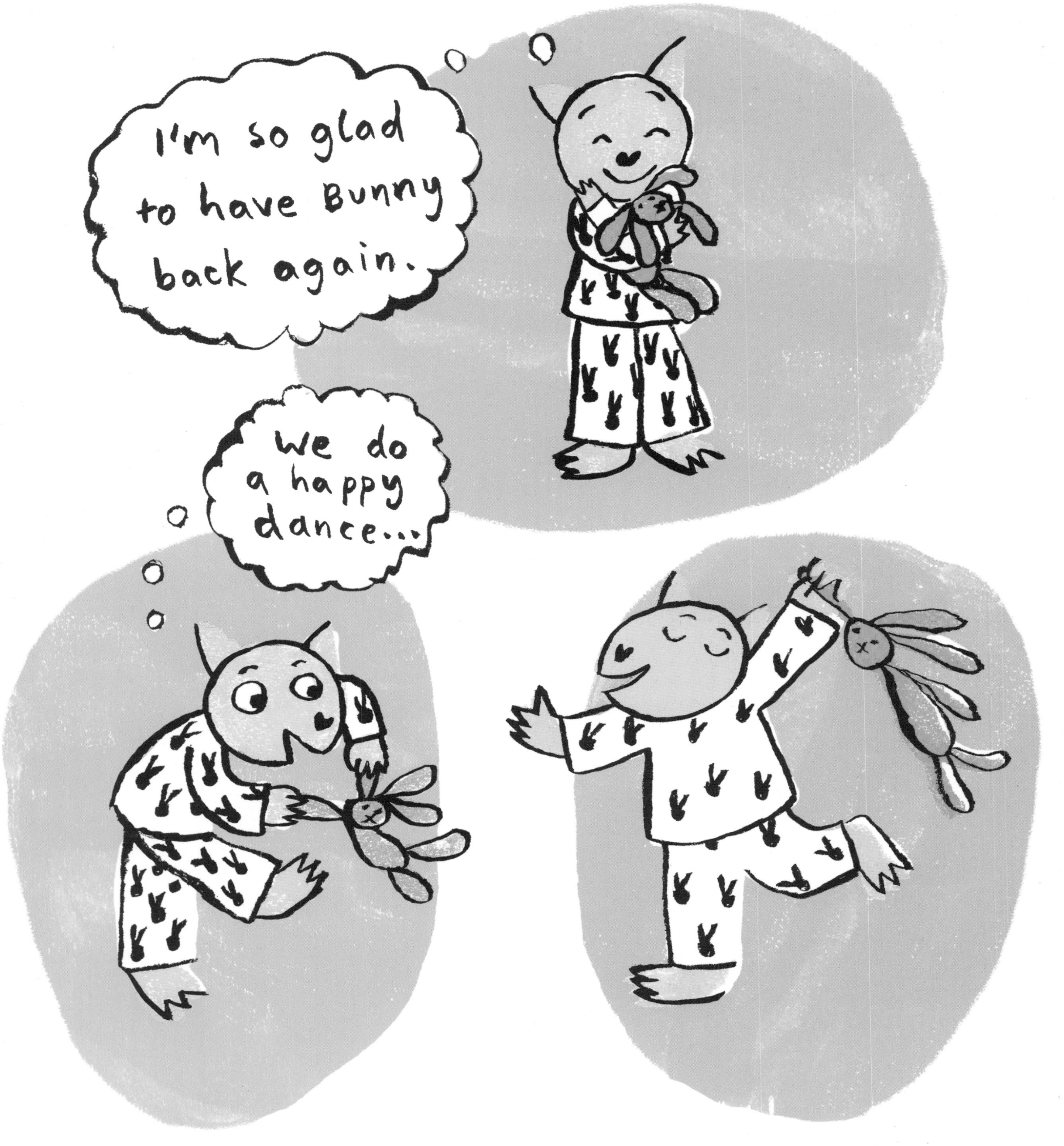
I'm so glad to have Bunny back again.
We do a happy dance...

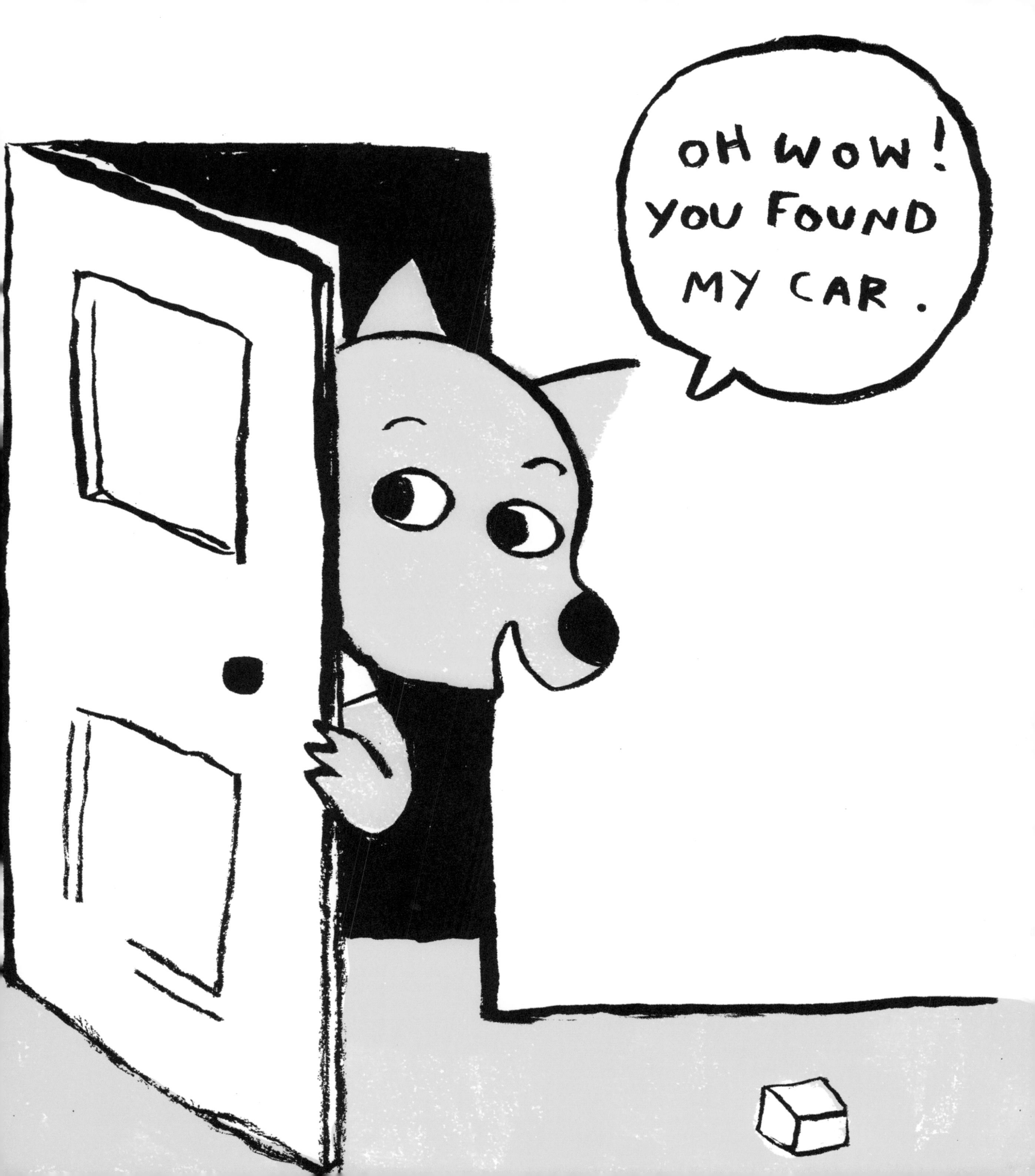
OH WOW! YOU FOUND MY CAR.